HODDER CHILDREN'S BOOKS

First published in Great Britain in 2020 by Hodder & Stoughton

1 3 5 7 9 10 8 6 4 2

Enid Blyton®, Enid Blyton's signature and The Magic Faraway Tree® are registered
trade marks of Hodder & Stoughton Limited
Text by Jeanne Willis © 2020 Hodder & Stoughton Limited
Illustrations by Mark Beech © 2020 Hodder & Stoughton Limited

A CIP catalogue record for this book is available from the British Library.

ISBN 978 1 444 95629 0

Printed and bound in China.

The paper and board used in this book are made from wood from responsible sources.

MIX
Paper from
responsible sources
FSC® C104740
FSC
www.fsc.org

Hodder Children's Books
An imprint of
Hachette Children's Group
Part of Hodder & Stoughton
Carmelite House
50 Victoria Embankment
London EC4Y 0DZ

An Hachette UK Company
www.hachette.co.uk
www.hachettechildrens.co.uk

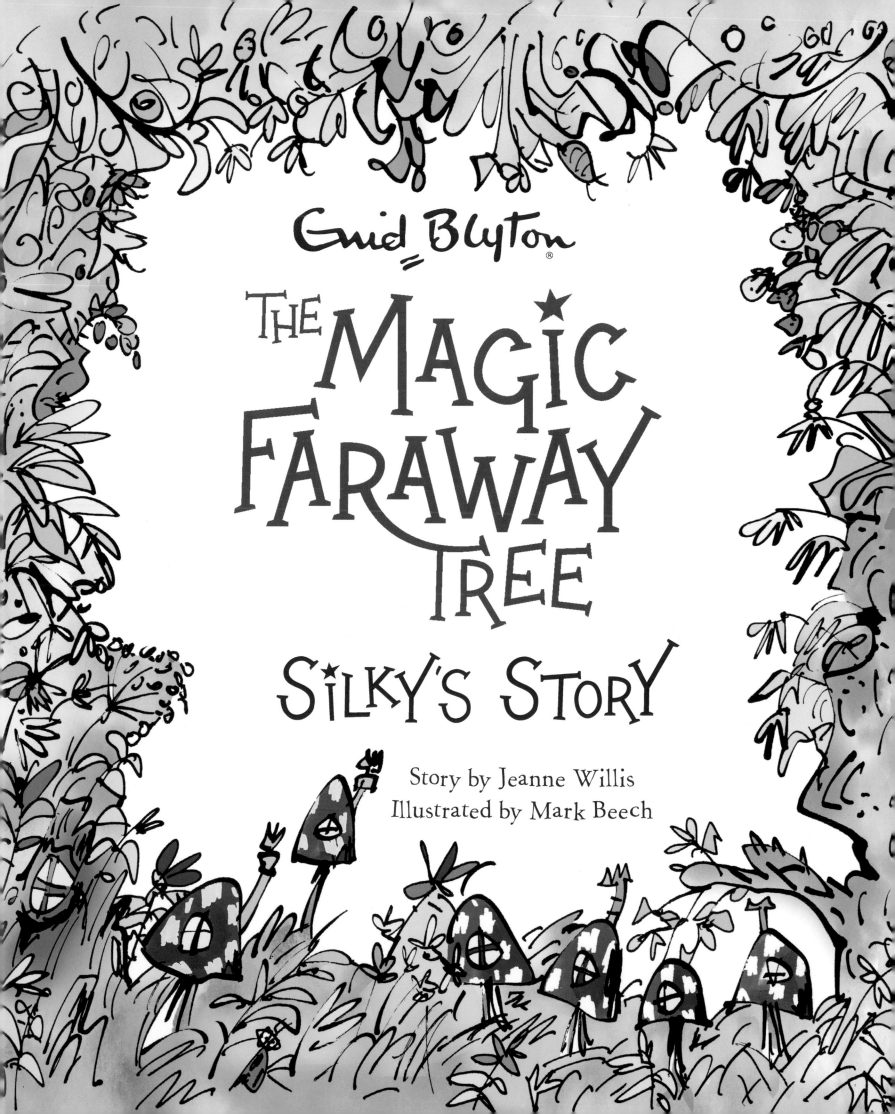

Enid Blyton®

THE MAGIC FARAWAY TREE

SILKY'S STORY

Story by Jeanne Willis

Illustrated by Mark Beech

Joe, Beth and Frannie were on their way to visit their favourite place in the world: the Magic Faraway Tree.

It was so tall, it touched the stars.

It grew all kinds of fruit and flowers.

At its top was a ladder leading
to amazing lands.

Most magical of all were the children's
special friends who lived in the Faraway Tree:

Moonface,

Saucepan Man

and Silky the Fairy.

"Let's all go up the Faraway Tree," said Frannie. "I'd love to show my new doll to Silky."

The Magic Faraway Tree
usually whispered

"Wisha-wisha-wisha"

but that day it was silent.
Something wasn't right.

"Why have the leaves
fallen off?" said Beth.

"And where is all the
delicious fruit?" asked
Frannie.

"It looks like it's been
eaten," said Joe.
"Even the prunes!"

"Let's ask Moonface. Perhaps he will know what has happened," said Beth. The children climbed the tree, following a trail of mess, mud and fruit stones.

They picked up clothes they found hanging in the branches on their way. Had someone lost their washing?

As they passed a little window in the tree trunk, they heard a shout.

"Argh!" screamed a pixie. "I thought you were the elephant!"

"The elephant?" exclaimed the children in surprise.

"Yes, there's a runaway elephant stampeding around the tree, making mischief," he grumbled.

He stared at the bundle of clothes. "Hey, those are my pants!"
Beth gave them to him and they carried on up the tree.

"Watch out," said Joe. "We're near Mrs Wash-a-lot's room in the tree. She always tips soapy water over us."

But Mrs Wash-a-lot had no water.

"The elephant drank it all!" she said. "It went trumpeting off, scattering all my clean laundry!"

When they arrived at Moonface's home, he wasn't there. But his bed was broken and it had huge footprints on the cover.

"Oh no, it looks as if the elephant has been here too," said Joe.

"Oh dear!" said Frannie. "Maybe Moonface has gone to see Silky?"

When they got to Silky's, a delicious smell of baking wafted out of the window. There were crumbs everywhere and Silky was nowhere to be seen.

But Moonface was there, looking very worried. Suddenly, they heard banging, crashing and shouting coming from above.

Looking up, they saw a little man covered in pots and pans that clattered together, climbing up the ladder.

"Hello, Saucepan Man! Why are you yelling?" said Joe.

"Why am I smelling?" he replied.

"He can't hear over the noise," giggled Beth. "What's the matter, Saucepan Man?"

"Want a natter?" he said. "This is no time to chat! The Land of Roundabouts and Swings has arrived."

"Good! It's fun there," said Frannie.

"Not anymore!" said Saucepan Man. "A wizard put a spell on an elephant from a roundabout and it came alive. It ate Silky's buns and stole her away! We must go and look for her."

"We need to find her before the land moves off again," said Joe. "Lead the way, Saucepan Man!"

The Land of Roundabouts and Swings seemed deserted.
    "Where is everybody?" said Joe.
    "Over there!" said Beth.
"Look, there's a crowd.
What are they staring at?"

It was an elephant!
It was sitting at the top of
the helter-skelter, holding
something small and sparkly
in its trunk.
"Can you see what it is,
Frannie?" said Joe.
But she had gone...

"Come down, Frannie!" shouted Joe but there was no reply. Beth and Joe waited anxiously with Moonface.

"What's happening?" said Joe.

"See for yourself," said Moonface, handing him his telescope.

"The elephant has Silky in his trunk!"
said Joe. "Oh no! What is Frannie doing?"

Frannie looked at the huge elephant.
"You've made a terrible mess,
frightened everyone
and you've taken our friend!" she said bravely.

"I was just looking for someone to play with!" he said sadly.

Then to the amazement of everyone watching, Frannie held out her doll. The elephant put Silky down gently and took the doll.

Frannie and Silky came whizzing back down the helter-skelter.

"Thank you for rescuing me," said Silky.

"You're welcome," said Frannie. "The elephant only wanted to play, so I gave it my doll instead of you."

"I'm so sorry I frightened you," said the elephant, trundling up beside them. "It's time for me to go back to the roundabout now. Would you all like a ride?"

As they came to the end of a wonderful turn on the carousel, they felt the wind begin to blow.

"That means the Land of Roundabouts and Swings is leaving," said Moonface. "We must go."

"Come to tea," said Silky. "The elephant ate my google buns but I have pop cakes."

"Hooray!" said the friends as they climbed down the ladder to Silky's house.

Saucepan Man sang
his tea-time song,

"Two pops
for a cake,

Two taps of
a spoon,

Two toots on
a kettle

And we'll be
home soon."

"Lovely pop cakes!" said Frannie.
"The honey just bursts into my mouth!"

"Glad you like them. And I'm sorry you
had to give your doll away," sighed Silky.

"Don't be sorry," said Frannie. "I'd much rather play
with a real fairy like you!"

The children waved
goodbye and slid
down the inside of the
Faraway Tree back to
the woods below.

"Wisha-wisha-wisha," whispered the Faraway Tree.

"The leaves have grown again!" said Beth. "This really is a magical place."

"Let's come back tomorrow," said Frannie. "Maybe there'll be a different land at the top of the tree!"